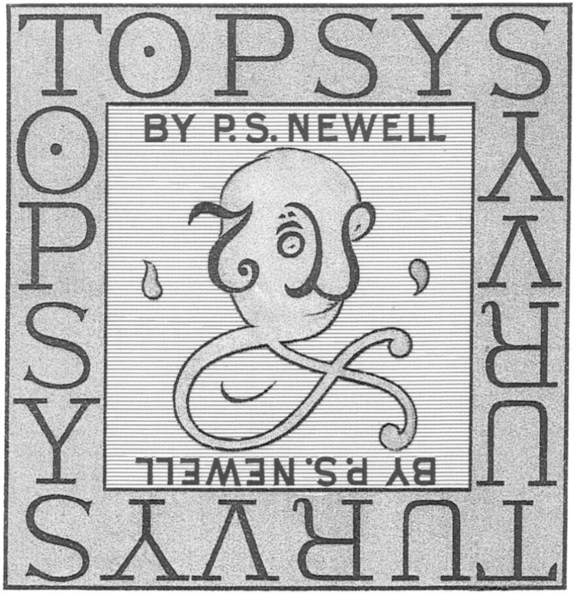

CHARLES E. TUTTLE COMPANY
RUTLAND · VERMONT   TOKYO · JAPAN

PUBLISHER'S FOREWORD

It is almost one hundred years since Peter Newell's enduringly popular *Topsys and Turvys 2* — the sequel to his bestselling *Topsys and Turvys* — was first published in the United States. Using the same ingenious style and imagination, he invents worlds of confusion and fun as he transforms hunters into bears, has a buffalo converse with a tree frog, or creates, and illustrates, pure nonsense.

These beautiful facsimile editions — both of which are newly republished by Charles E. Tuttle — reproduce all of the brilliant color and charm of the originals, and will ensure that *Topsys and Turvys* can be shared and enjoyed anew by future generations.

Peter Newell (1862–1924) began his career as an artist drawing portraits, using crayons as his medium. In his fantastic humor, many believe, is the first appearance of the gentle humor of the absurd which *The New Yorker* has subsequently developed to such a high level.

In addition to the two *Topsys and Turvys*, Peter Newell wrote and illustrated many other books for children, including *The Hole Book* (1908), *The Slant Book* (1910), and *The Rocket Book* (1912) (all also published by Charles E. Tuttle), which are equally inventive and remain popular bestsellers. He also illustrated many classic works, including Mark Twain's *Innocents Abroad*, and an edition of Lewis Carroll's *Alice's Adventures in Wonderland* which caused a great controversy at the time. All are characterized by his brilliant imagination and originality which, it might be said, comes straight from the minds of the children for whom he drew so well.

But found the little manikin could well defend himself.

A wicked robber horseman charged upon a woodland elf,

They heard a flock of booby-birds come whirring through the air.

Beneath their big and shady hats the bathers had a scare—

And looking rather sad because he 's lost his fattened pig.

Here is a German farmer dressed in a curious rig,

Till—bang!—his magazine blew up and hurled the crew in air.

The Malay pirate eyed his foes in hopeless fierce despair

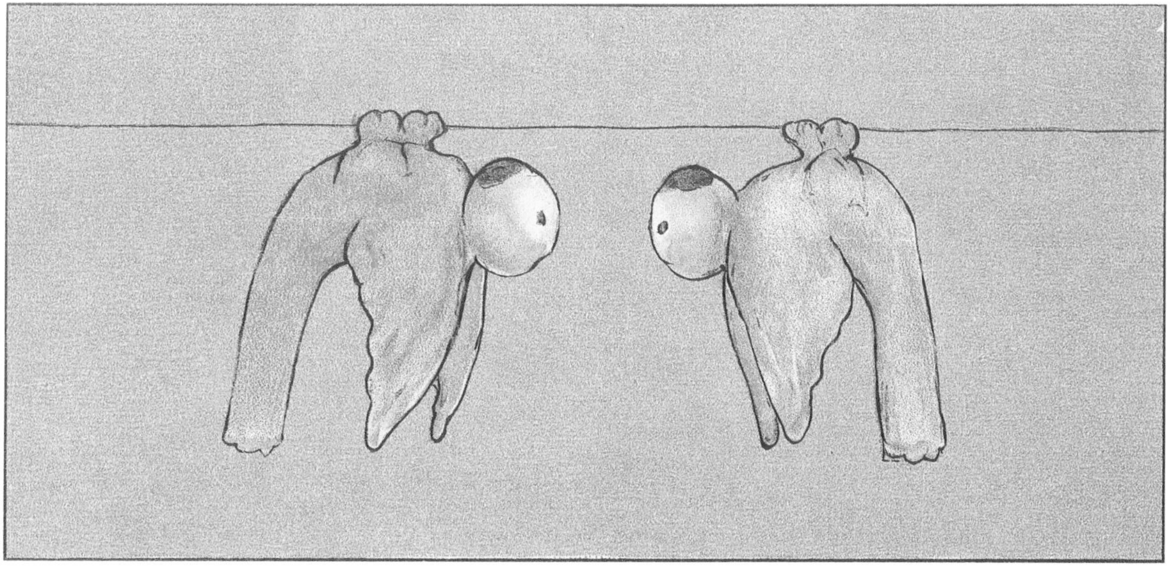

Upon a line, two Japanese, though dolls, are most polite;

Not like these shrieking parrakeets, both spoiling for a fight.

A lion made an end of her—she came too near the shore.

The swan was swimming on a stream where oft she 'd been before.

That night this grinning nightmare came, and made poor Pompey groan.

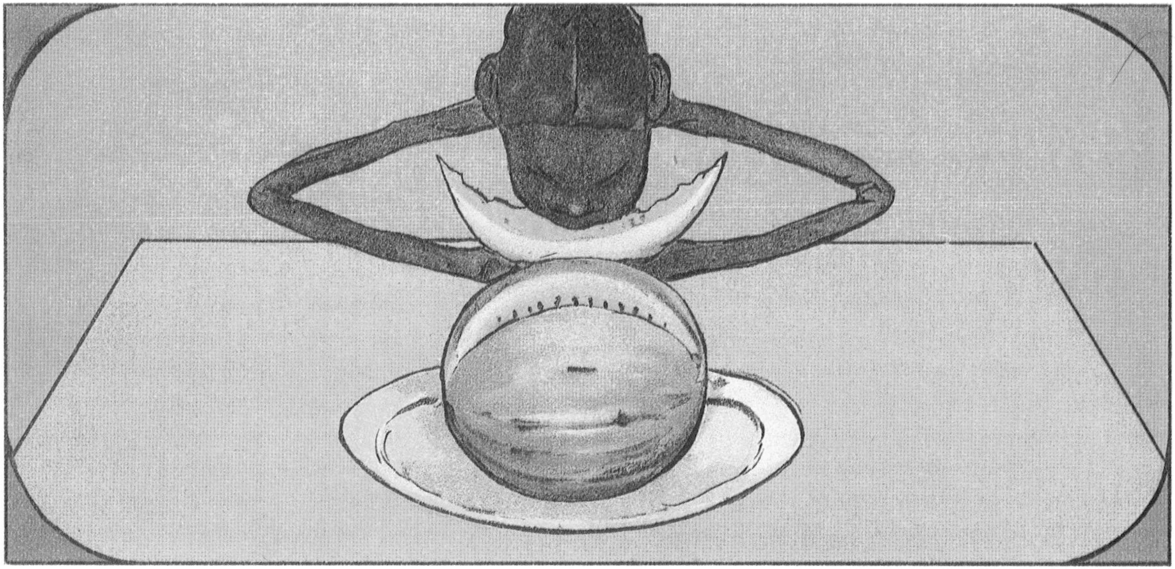

A watermelon Pompey loves, and ate one all alone.

But meanwhile came this greedy duck, and *she* the apple found.

"I 'll come again," the small bird said, before the apple round;

But by their clothes they saw a snake, when they came to the shore.

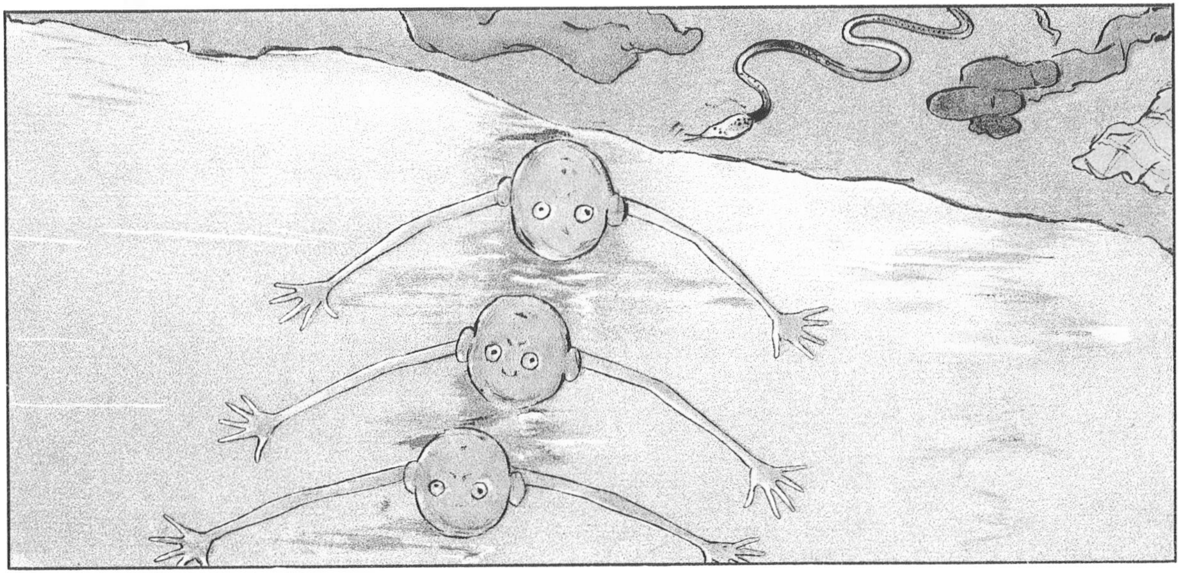

Three country boys went swimming, where oft they 'd been before;

The gardener set his choicest ferns where they would get the sun.

And upside down, upon their stalks, they took a little run.

He lost the gnat, but found this spring. It came up to his neck.

A broad-brimmed sage once chased a gnat, a tiny harmless speck.

The twins their Tam o' Shanters don, jump in and off they ride.

Before the house a cart is seen, a hat hung at each side.

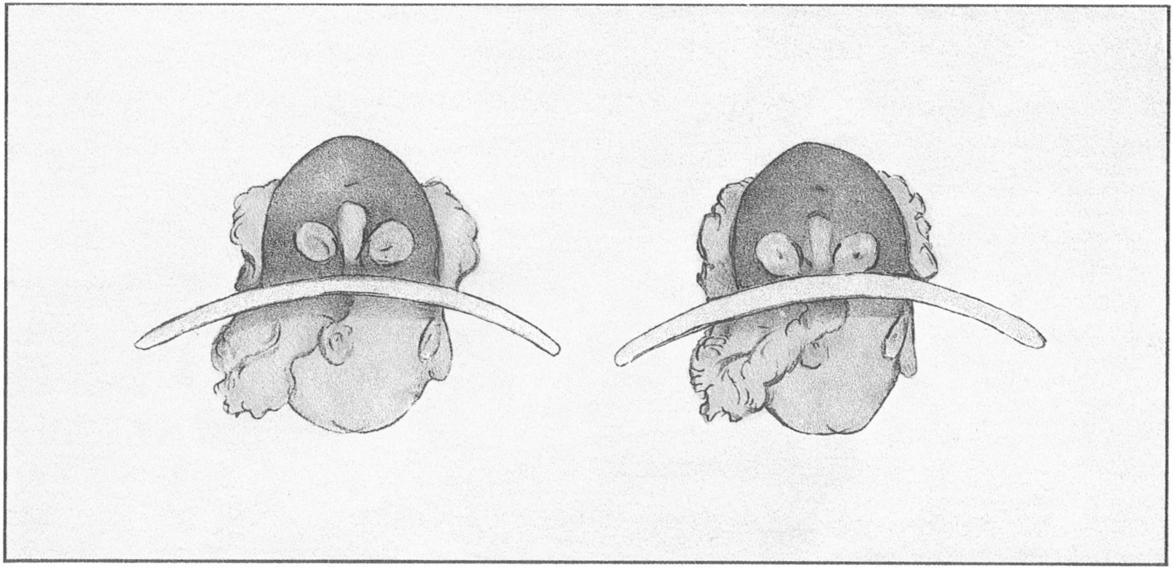

In town the Hickson girls are fair, with lips as red as cherries;

But when they linger by the sea they tan as brown as berries.

He gave a fling, and found the fish was hanging in a tree.

"I 've hooked a fish!" cries hasty Hugh: "I 'll land him, too. Now see!"

You see, it was a Spring lamb, and jumped the fence, no doubt.

The shepherd 's looking for the lamb. "How did that lamb get out?"

Has paused to see this monstrous snake just crawling from the bog.

A Bengal-tiger, lurking behind a fallen log,

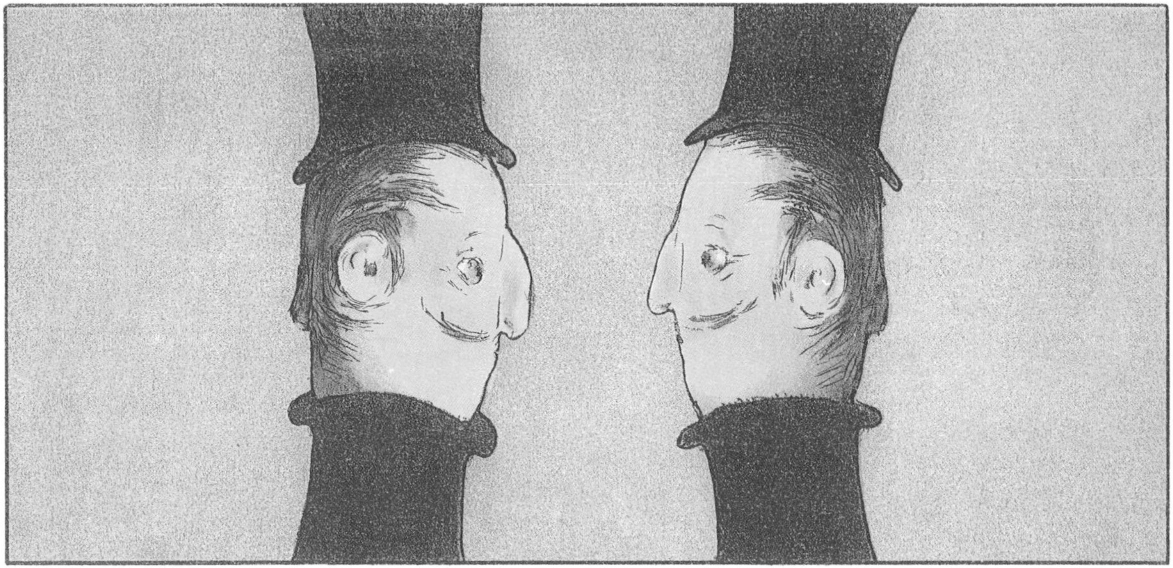

Two "chappies" on the avenue one foggy day did meet,

And side by side, with eye-glass fixed, they strolled along the street.

When oh! a monster bird swooped down and seized him in its bill.

Within his skiff young Izaak sat, fishing with joy and skill,

This shepherd thought poetic thoughts as by the flocks he sat;

But while he wrote his verses, the goat fed on his hat.

And so their hats they set afloat, and each one climbed aboard.

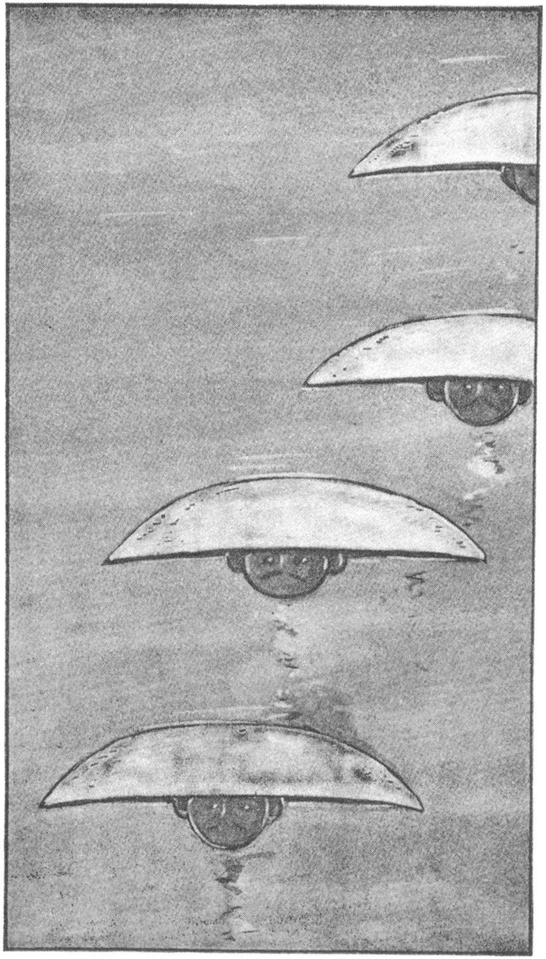

Some Japs in wicker hats once found a stream too deep to ford,

And James Broadbrim, a Quaker slim, the same brave feat essays.

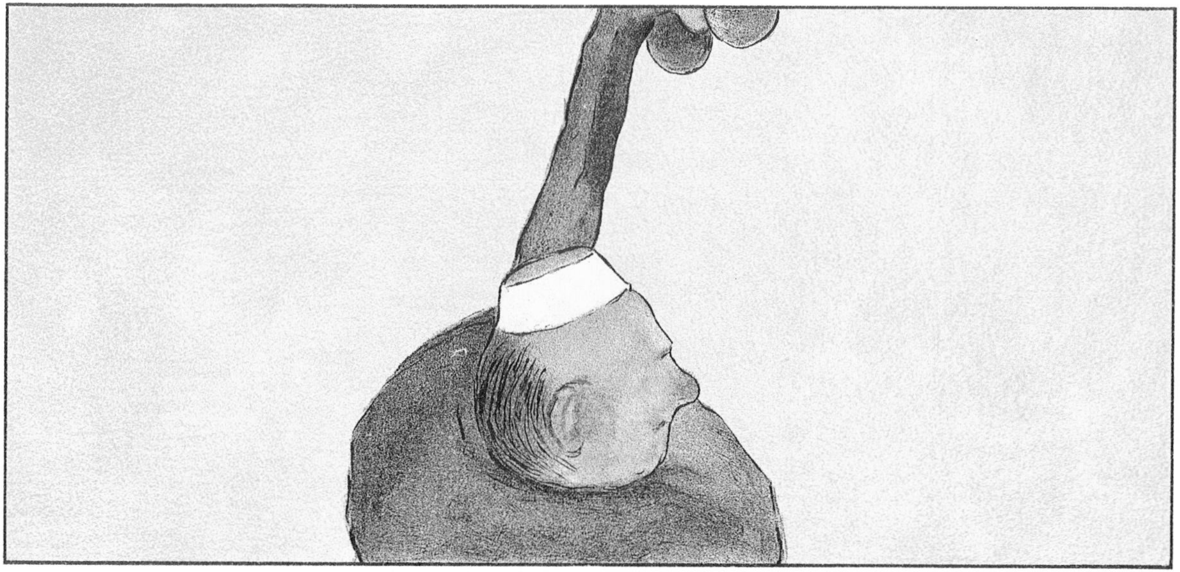

John Stout his tissues to reduce a dumb-bell thus does raise.

Fer massy sakes!—a monst'us frog! Young Sambo put dat dah."

"Dah 's sunthin' curus in my hat,—it 's movin', I declah.

Here Simon Grimm lies fast asleep, within his cozy bed;

And now a stealthy robber comes, a slouch-hat on his head.

But in a tree the wildcat hid until he went away.

A hunter wandered through the wood in search of lurking prey ;

Because they know three hunting-dogs are close upon their trail.

Why do these scurrying, frightened hares come coursing through the vale?

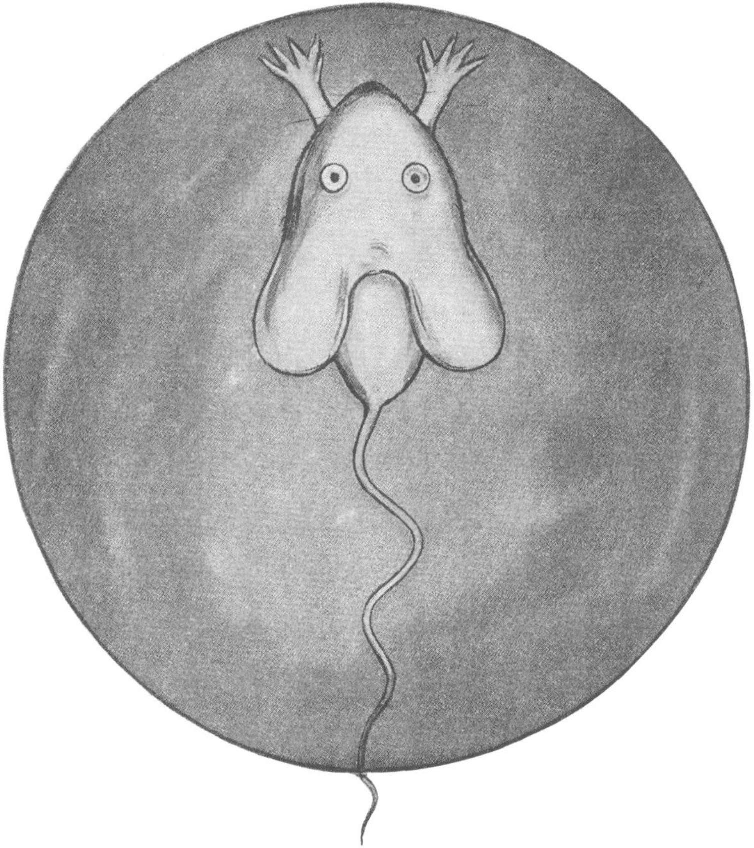

A drop of water magnified this creature queer reveals;

And look!—a microscopic mouse after the fellow steals!

But when the mother bear returned, he fled his life to save.

The hunter found two bear-cubs and took them from their cave,

But take to flight when on the bank rhinoceroses greet.

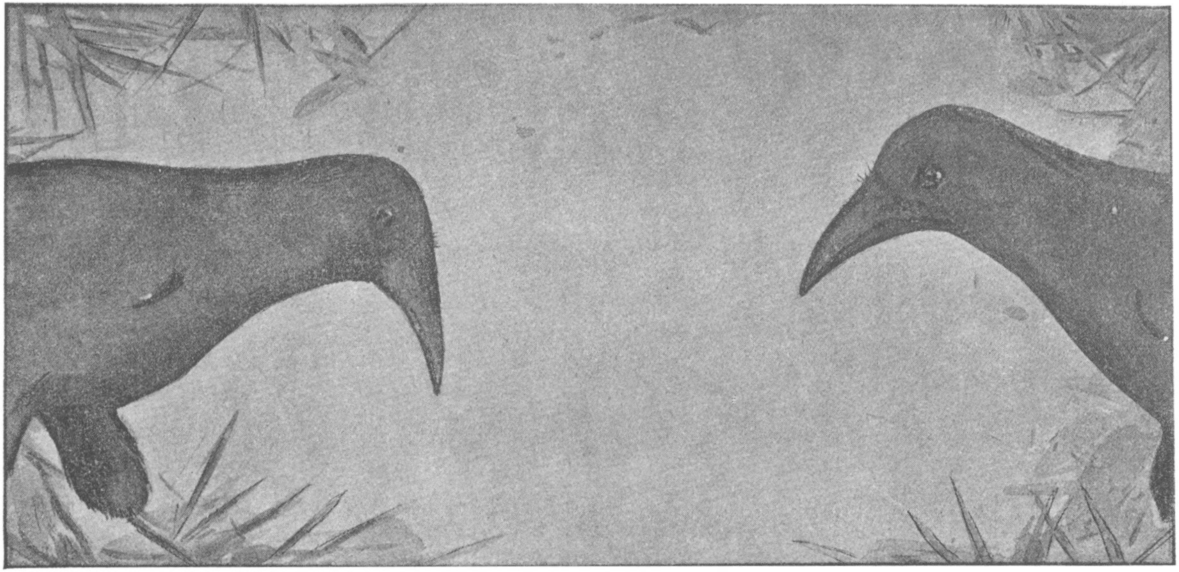

With cheerful caws two inky crows beside a river meet,

They missed their aim, and not a bird of all the flock was caught.

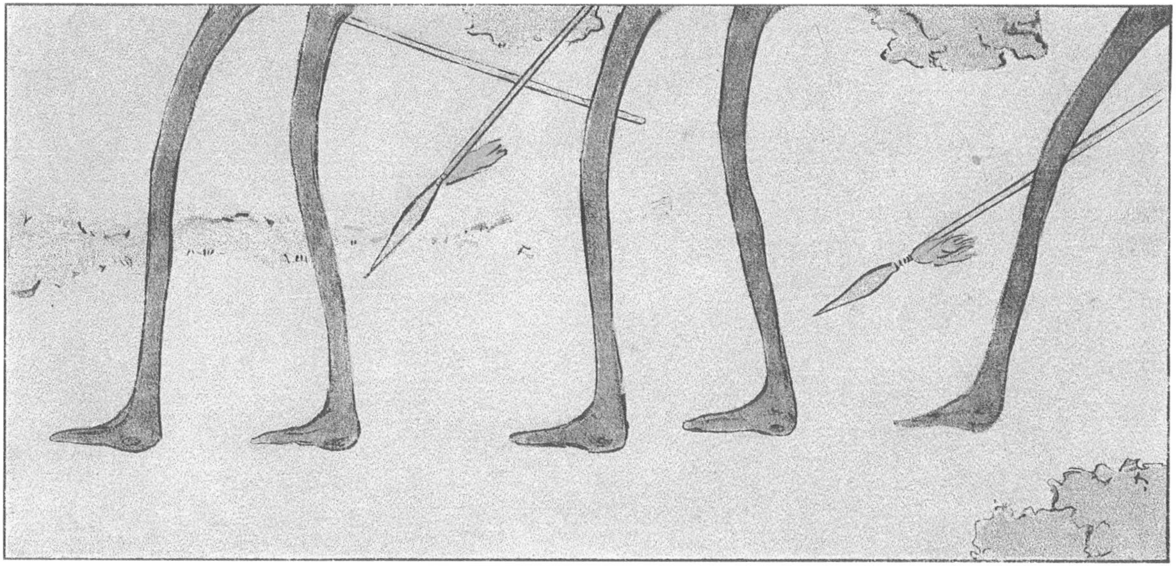

Some ostrich-hunters with their spears set out in search of sport;

Here are the fish they did n't catch, and now you may decide.

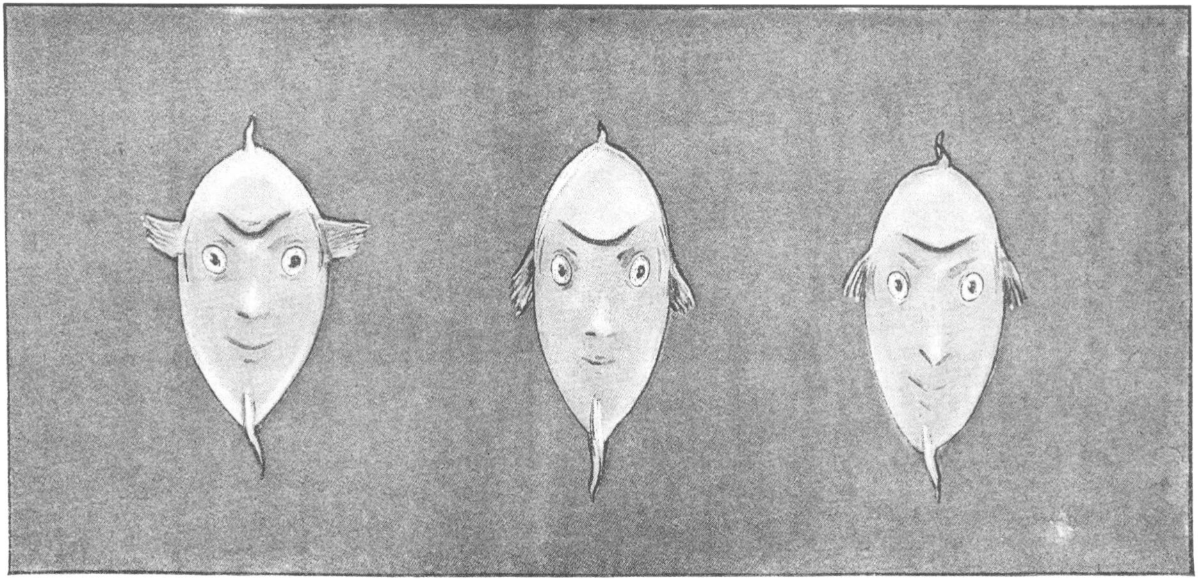

"The fish were bigger than our heads," they vowed.—"yes, twice as wide"

Above his lair a hawk is perched, but poised for instant flight.

Hid in a nook the panther sleeps, and hunts for prey by night;

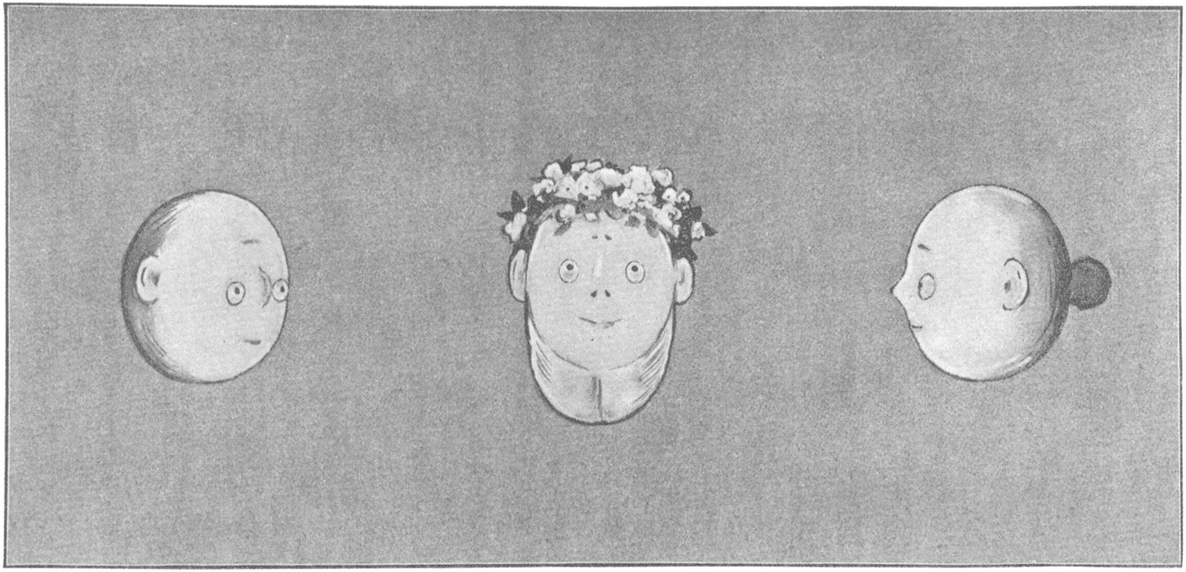

When on the May Queen's golden curls the pretty wreath was laid

It slipped down over head and ears, so large it had been made.

But when she sang a solo she did not look so sweet.

To singing-school Belinda went, in costume new and neat,

Till brave Ah Boo came toddling up and put the beast to flight.

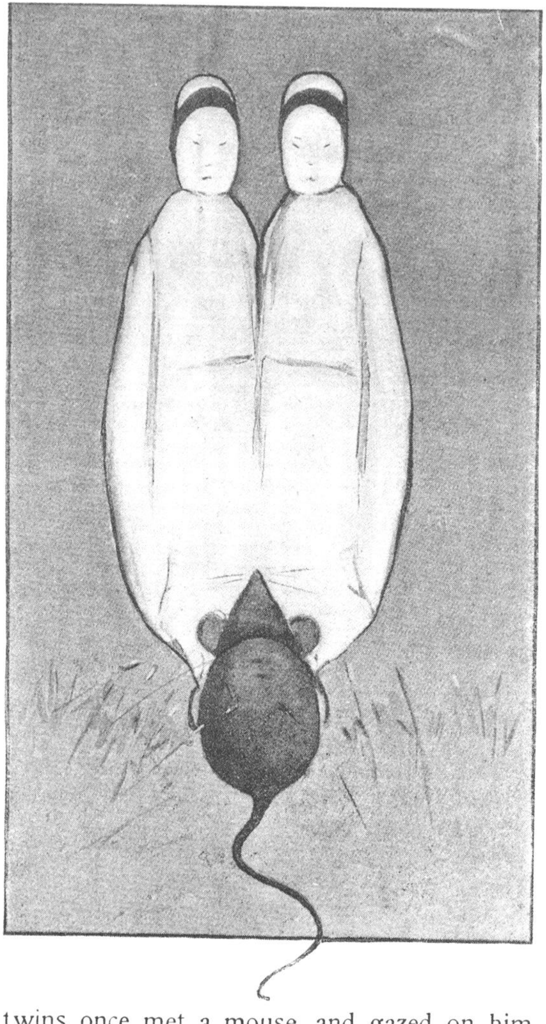

Two Chinese twins once met a mouse, and gazed on him with fright,

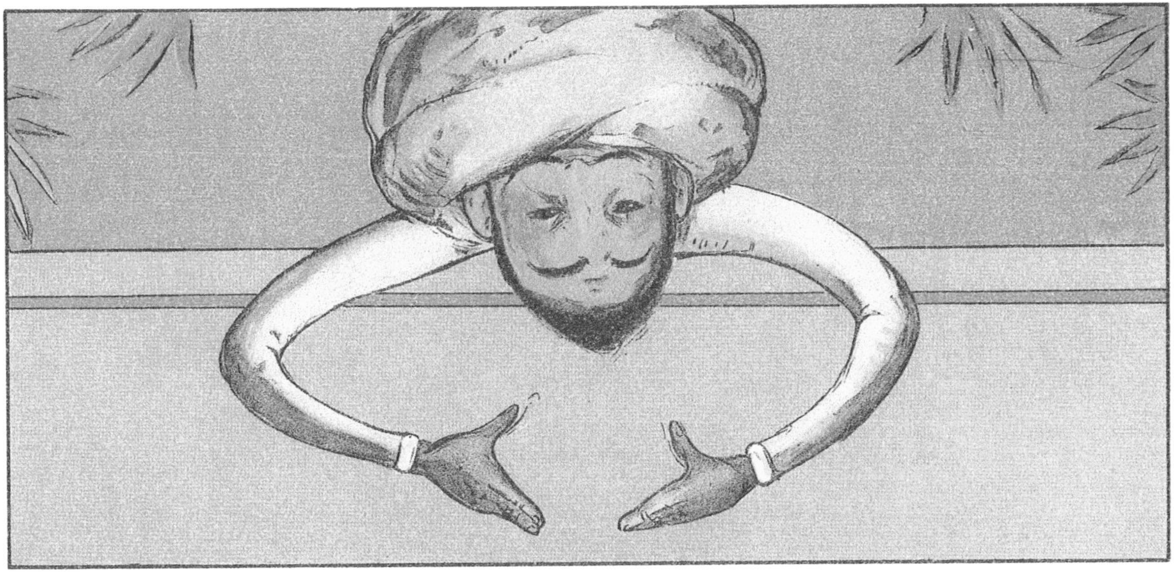

This is the serpent-charmer so brave he never quakes

When twice around his neck are wound two lively, squirming snakes.

So low that Rudolph could n t get down to it at all.

They played a match at tennis, and Charlie served the ball

Unto the dentist, who exclaims, "I 'll take it out, of course!"

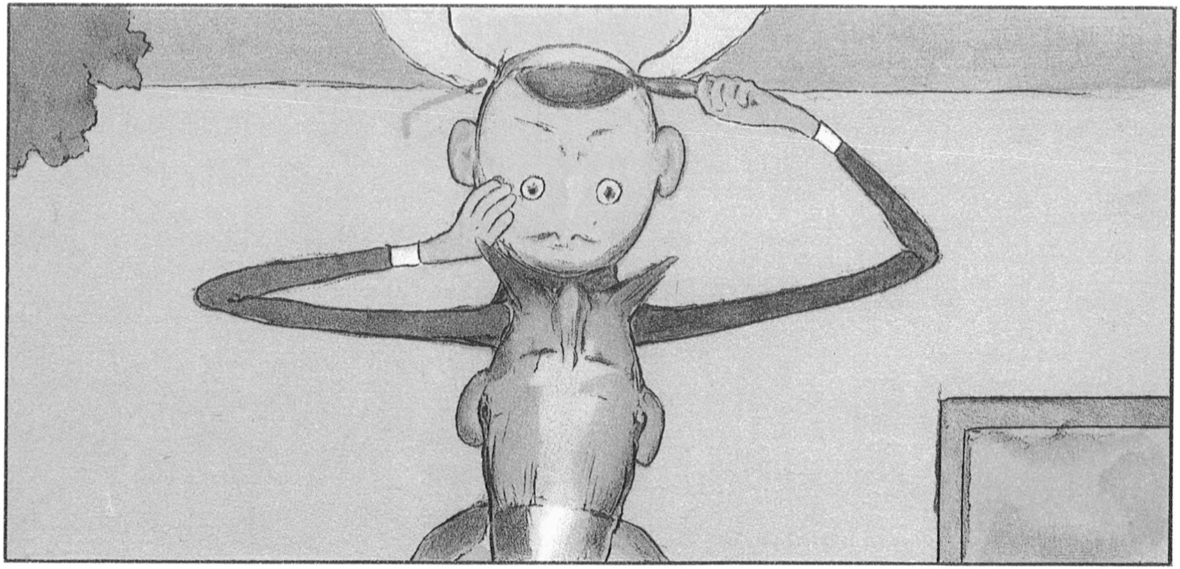

"Oh, my poor tooth!" the rider groans, and urges on his horse

“You ’re flat!” remarked the buffalo, and left him with a sneer.

A tree-toad, perched upon a tree, was piping loud and clear;

But when a polar-bear arrived, the man took to his heels.

In pointed hat the Eskimo was on the watch for seals;

But near the stream a long-legged stork secured a breakfast first.

Down to the river crawled a snake, meaning to quench his thirst;

In hope of pork, two small gray wolves watched all one autumn day;

But Piggy smelled a rat (or wolf), and went another way.

His fine long-eared retriever plunged in and quickly got it.

A duck came flying o'er the pond; and when the sportsman shot it,

John Wilson's father, grave and stern, is sorely grieved to see

That scapegrace John 's been robbing his choicest apple-tree.

The people in the windows their keen amusement show,

To see these Jacks-in-boxes exhibited below.

And slides headforemost down the hill when Winter brings the snow.

In shady groves Adolphus swings when Summer's zephyrs blow,

So clumsy were Jan's wooden shoes that in the pond he tumbled

While driving geese, and how they squawked to see Jan's pride thus humbled!

Only his head and hands are seen, he sinks so very deep.

The rancher in the blizzard goes out to save his sheep,

"Meow-meow! Pfitz-pfitz!—at me," says Mrs. Bulger's cat.

"Bow-wow! Wow-woof!" says Bulger's dog. What is he barking at?

And in their town the Woollyheads with fierce defiance shout.

The British fire a volley, behind their strong redoubt;

The patient twins are waiting within their cradle deep

Until their nurse, kind Hannah, comes, to rock them both to sleep.

A famous warrior of that land is ever in her head.

Here is a lady of Japan, and at the court, 't is said,

Here 's Uncle Ike, and Auntie Jane, the wife of Uncle Ike,

But which is which? It seems to me they 're very much alike.

But, on my feet again, I saw this Owl so wise and meek.

I stood upon my head and saw this strange two-headed freak;

Whether the musk-ox wears his horns in a becoming fashion.

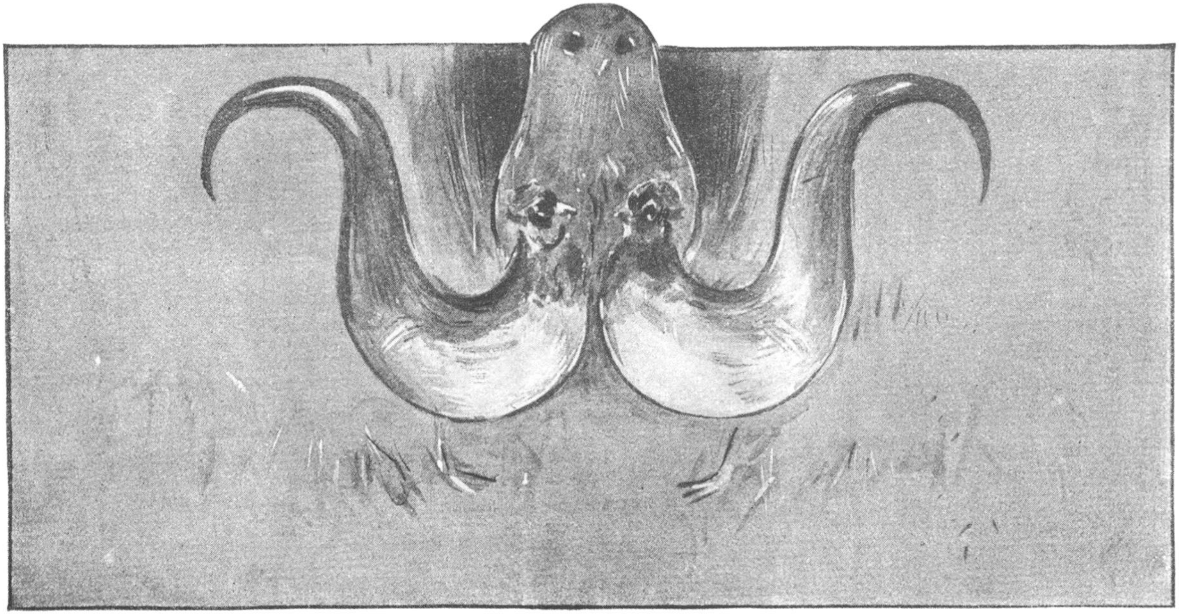

The owl looks on while fowls discuss till both are in a passion

And then his old hen sat in it, and used it for a nest.

Old Jerry wore his hat so long that it became a jest;

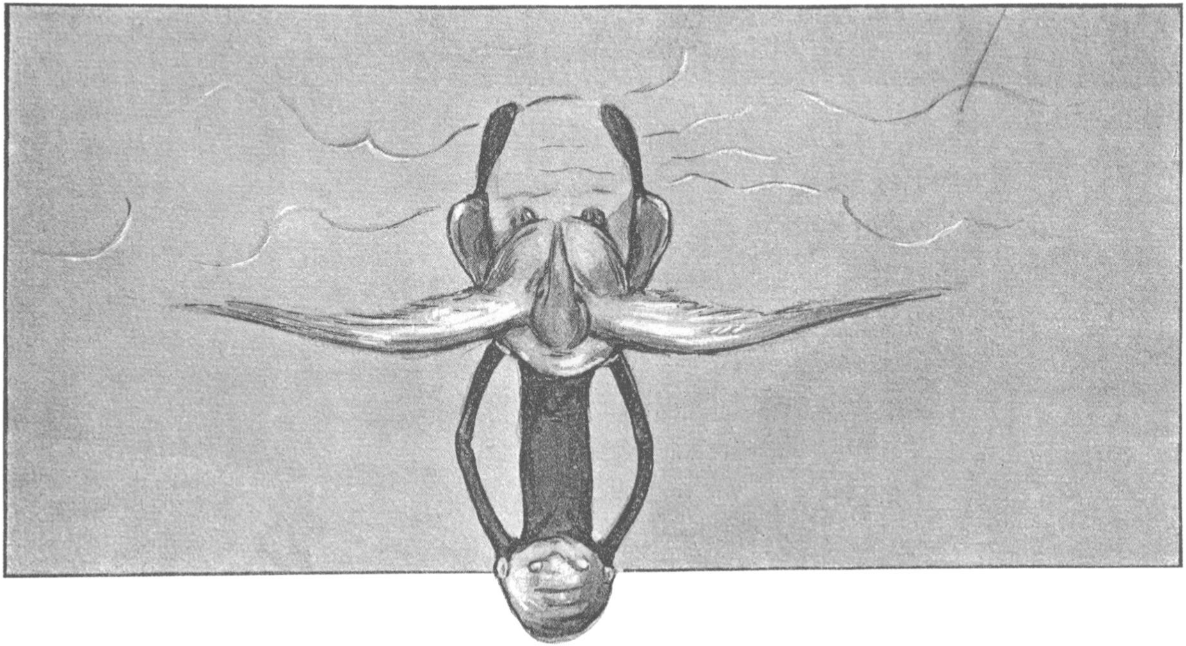

"Where is your son, now, Captain Blobbs? I hear he is away."

"I sent him off upon a lark; he won't be back to-day."

He plumps a big one in his mouth, and finds it very good.

The hungry tramp has come upon some cherries in the wood;

"I saw a pretty boy, but not like you that I could see."

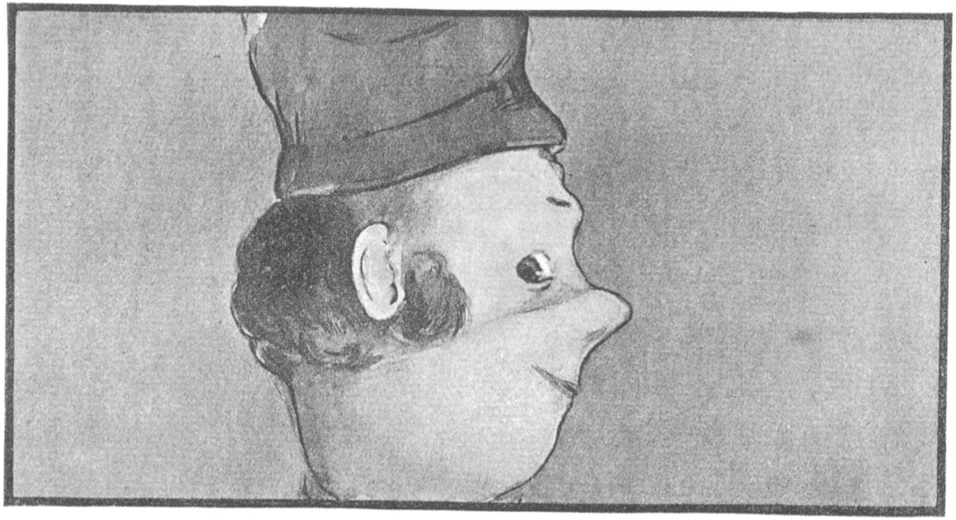

"Oh, have you seen my little boy?—he looks not unlike me."

The banker balanced all his books, and then—the story goes—

He was so pleased he balanced them again, upon his nose.

Jack Frost has nipped the leaves and brought the acorns tumbling down.

The acorns now are falling—the leaves are turning brown;

At sight of this forbidding tramp, the barber has a scare,

But finds it is a customer who says: "Please cut my hair."

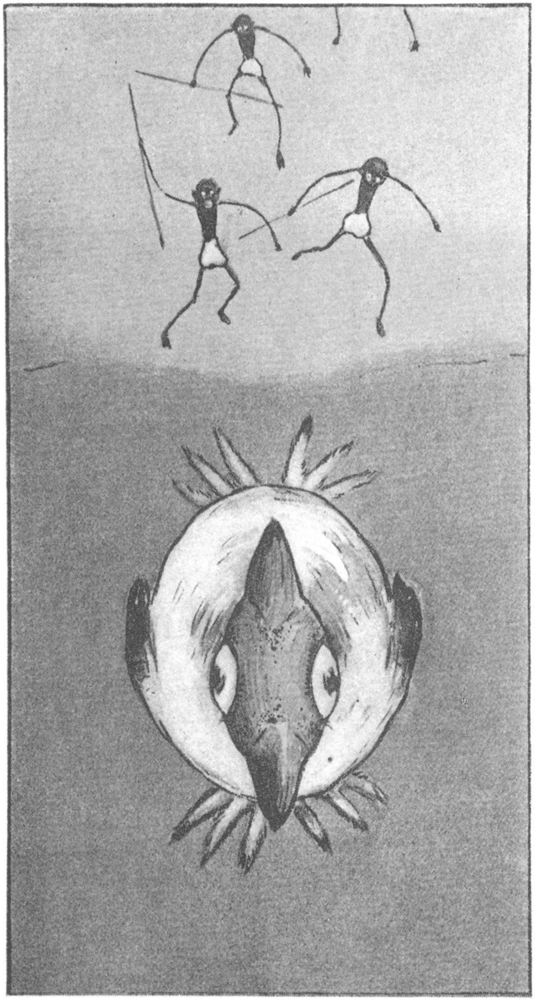

Some natives found a whang-bird's trail and followed on its tracks.

But when the whang-bird turned at bay, they all fell on their backs.

The squirrel gazed with wonder upon his gloomy face.

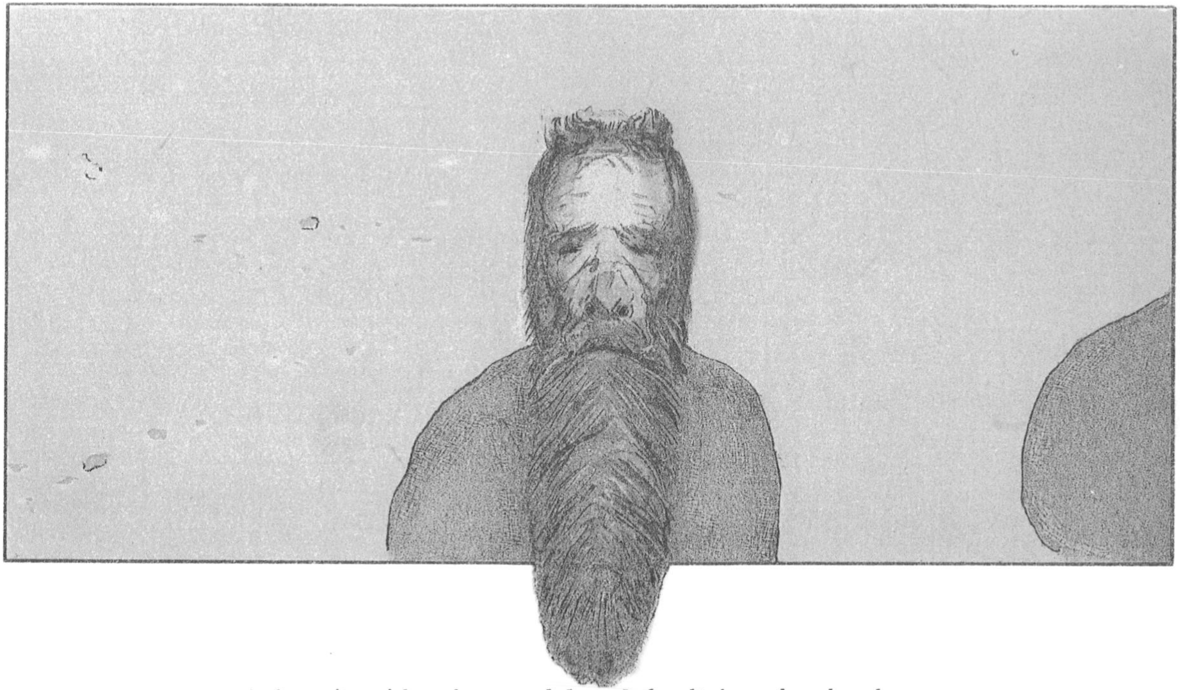

A hermit with a long red beard dwelt in a lonely place;

Until the shark came gliding up, and put him out of sight.

The captain's pig fell overboard and swam with all his might,

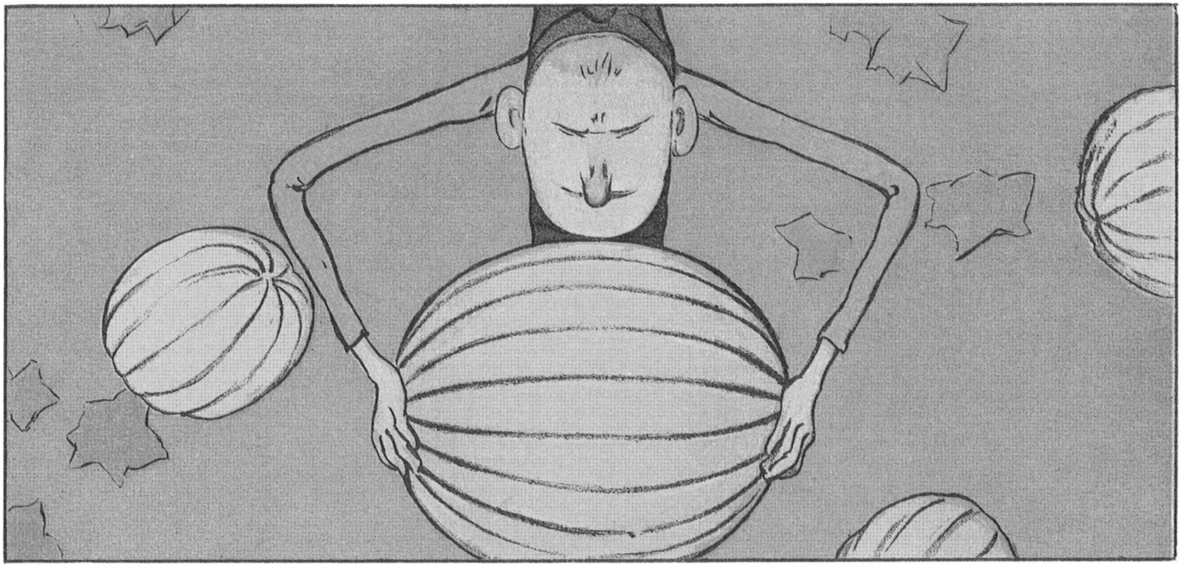

Farmer Grumpkins raised some pumpkins; and one day this fall

He raised a hundred-pounder, and did n't mind at all.

It ran upon a hidden mine, which blew the launch sky high!

The rebel launch escaped the shell, but ere it could reply

While, just behind, a countryman undue surprise displayed.

A foreigner in curious clothes sat resting in the shade,

And here 's the awful thing they found—a donkey munching leaves.

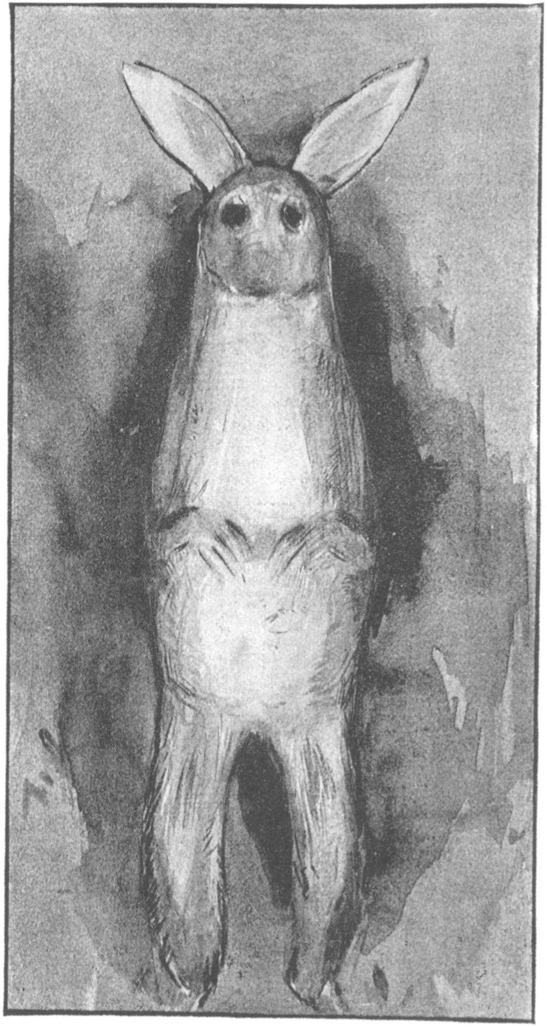

"I hear a noise!" the hare exclaimed. "Oh—murder, fire, *thieves!*"

This book is like a tumbler. It 's thus that you begin it,

But till it is inverted, there 's always more within it.

REPRESENTATIVES

British Isles & Continental Europe:
SIMON & SCHUSTER INTERNATIONAL GROUP, London
Australasia: BOOKWISE INTERNATIONAL
1 Jeanes Street, Beverley, 5009, South Australia

Published by the Charles E. Tuttle Company, Inc.
of Rutland, Vermont & Tokyo, Japan
with editorial offices at
Suido 1-chome, 2-6, Bunkyo-ku, Tokyo

Library of Congress Catalog Card No. 87-51208
International Standard Book No. 0-8048-1552-6

First published by The Century Co., 1894
First Tuttle edition, 1988

Printed in Japan